Mental Block

A novella by

Mary Farias

IrisBlu publishing
Tucson, Arizona

First printing 2019

ISBN 978-0-9843406-7-5

For all of my older gymnasts who have courageously fought a mental block and won: you're not alone. This one's for you!

Introduction

Gymnastics is difficult. Little kids just don't know it yet. For a lot of them, when they come into the sport, obtaining and maintaining skills is easy: they learn a forward roll or a cartwheel when they're three, four, or five, and they practice it all day, everyday, in the gym, in the living room, in the grass, on the playground. They seem to only get better and better, stronger and stronger.

Most competitive gymnasts start out this way. However, by the time that these gymnasts reach sixth, seventh, eighth grade, and especially high school, things begin to get difficult. No longer are they the tiny little kids who run and jump and "play" gymnastics. Their bodies begin to grow and change. Their minds begin to play tricks on them.

Some of these older gymnasts begin to form a love-hate relationship with the sport. Gone are the days of simple bliss. Now are the days of aches, pains, fears; things get complicated. These older gymnasts still love the sport, and they want to achieve their goals. They want to continue to get better, but some days, their bodies just won't let them. They'd like to get up on the bar and swing with ease like they did one year or even six months ago, but it just doesn't feel the same. Their center of gravity has changed, their height has changed, their strength has changed.

This new series of books is for precisely those gymnasts: those who grew up knowing that gymnastics was their life, those who are dedicated to the sport, but now are faced with different challenges: height, weight, high school, friends, boys, homework, and everything that accompanies being an older gymnast.

I have a number of older gymnasts in my gym, and I am proud of each one. They are all strong and wonderful gymnasts in their own right, and they all have their own set of circumstances, each gymnast unique, and each one growing into better and more beautiful people because of them. The struggles they encounter now will not only make them stronger gymnasts, but they will make them better problem solvers, more self-confident, and more independent people with greater self-esteem. They will be better equipped to handle any challenge they may encounter as they grow up.

As a coach, I believe it is my calling to help all of my gymnasts face their obstacles head on, and not give up. Don't get me wrong: I don't believe that all gymnasts will stay in the sport forever. Inevitably, girls will retire. But I can help them look back on the sport with a smile and the knowledge that they gave it everything they had.

I'm proud of my older gymnasts: they are positive role models for my younger gymnasts coming up, and the lessons they learn now will help them in all of life's adventures.

Enjoy!
Mary

Mental Block

Mental Block

Dear Diary,

Gymnastics is going awesome! Everyday I have been getting my workouts finished quickly so I can work upgrades as much as possible. I want to be in the next group ASAP and get closer to Becca and Liz's level. They are so good! Today at practice I felt bad because I wanted to get my work done on beam, but Erica wanted to tell me a story about what happened at school. It's hard to have a best friend who doesn't take gymnastics as seriously as I do. I feel bad saying that, but I don't think she does. I want to be GOOD! But I also don't want to make Erica feel bad, because she is my best friend. I'll just keep doing what I'm supposed to at practice, and hopefully Erica will catch on...

All for now. Bed time!

Allison and Erica had ten pull-ups in mixed grip left. “Come on, Erica! You can do it!” encouraged Allison. Erica pulled down on the bar to get her chin above it. She winced and she swung a little to complete number ten.

“Ok. Your turn,” she said, breathless.

Allison jumped up to the high bar, switched her right hand to under grip, and squeezed her legs together. Her toes were pointed as she pulled down on the bar to complete her pull-ups. “Good job, Al,” said Erica.

“Thanks,” Allison answered. “Forty pull-ups is tough to do!” Part of the conditioning for Allison’s team was to do ten pull-ups in each grip: regular, under grip, mixed grip with the right hand in under grip, and then mixed grip with the left hand in under grip. Some struggled and had spot, and all of them were breathing hard and shaking out their hands by the end of it.

After conditioning, the team stretched before going home for the night. Jean walked over to Allison’s group with a younger girl following her. They had never seen her before.

“Girls, this is Katie. She’s going to be trying out at The Gymnastics Club starting tomorrow. She just finished competing level 5 at her old gym. Let’s all make her feel welcome.”

Allison was the first in line to say, “Hey, Katie. Welcome to TGC! I’m sure you’re going to love it here.”

“Thanks,” Katie said quietly, her eyes darting down to the floor.

After they finished stretching, the team walked together through the gym to the locker room. While they gathered their things, they chattered about what they were going to wear to school the next day, and the homework they had to finish when they got home. Jean walked Katie out to her mom in the lobby. The other coaches waited for all the girls to walk out of the gym before they went to the office to pack up their things to leave.

"How was practice today?" Allison's mom smiled as her gymnast hopped in the front seat.

"It went really well. Jean had me working aerials on beam after I finished my assignment."

"Wow! Were you able to do it?"

"Yeah, I worked my way up to the low beam with mats on the sides. I landed on the beam on a few of them."

"Nice work," Allison's mom said as they pulled out of the parking lot.

"A new girl is starting tomorrow in the group right below mine. Her name is Katie. She seems really quiet."

"I'm sure she's just nervous," Allison's mom replied. "Give her time. She'll warm up."

On school nights after practice, it was all business. Practice ended at 8:00, and it took about 20 minutes to get home. Allison barged through the front door, yelled, "Hi Dad!" and ran up the stairs. She took a shower while her parents finished getting dinner on the table. Allison ate her dinner, then finished the rest of her homework before going to bed, hopefully by 10:00. At least, that was her goal.

After her shower, Allison went downstairs to the kitchen. Pasta with white beans and vegetables waited for her at the table. Her parents were cleaning up the kitchen. "How was practice, Pumpkin?" her dad asked.

"It went well," Allison said between bites. "I did aerials on beam."

"I have no idea what that is, but it sounds pretty cool!"

"It's a no-handed cartwheel."

"On the *beam*?" Her dad's eyes grew wide.

Allison smiled as she put a chunk of broccoli in her mouth. She finished eating and brought her bowl to the sink.

"Night, Mom. Night, Dad."

"Night, Hun. Are you finished with your homework?" her mom asked.

"I just have some reading to finish up."

"Okay. Get it done."

Allison went upstairs to brush her teeth. She thought about her aerials and felt nervous and excited at the same time. She looked forward to getting back into the gym to do them again tomorrow!

Mental Block

The next day at gym, Allison and her group went to bars. Their assignment was on the white board:

Warm-up:

3 x 3 K CHS K LB 3 K CHS K HB

2 x 25 hollow-arch taps

3 x 5 tap swings

Workout:

3 x 5 giants

5 KCHS FH HS LB or HB

5 dismounts

5 releases

5 1/2 pirouettes

Allison read over the workout and planned where she would do each piece. She would do the kip cast handstand kips on the two competition bar sets, the hollow-arch taps on the recreational set of bars, and the tap swings on the single rail and uneven bar sets. That would take six turns, with the hollow-arches in the middle on an open bar. Then she could get started on her workout.

The work didn't phase Allison; it was the job she was tasked to do for the day. And it was just like any other Thursday; no routines today, just skills. She chalked her grips and looked for the nearest open bar set.

As she walked over to do her turn, she spotted Katie doing a flawless press handstand on the floor. From a seated straddle position, Katie pushed off the floor, leaning her shoulders over her hands, she pushed through them and pressed her body up, just barely missing her perfectly pointed toes on the floor. She straddled her legs up and brought them together in handstand, which she held for a good three seconds. Then she straddled her legs, leaned her shoulders over her hands, and returned to a straddle sit. Most of the girls in her group had trouble getting to handstand, let alone coming back down with control. This girl was good!

"She's amazing!" Erica said. "She has perfect posture and form and she's so young!"

"Yeah, she looks pretty good. I wonder what she's working on for next year." Katie had just finished competing in the fall season at her old gym. The Gymnastics Club, however, competed in a different league, USAIGC, so their season was just about to start. Their main focus was routines for the next 5-6 months, which left just a little time for higher-level skills. In fact, their first meet was in a few weeks!

Standing in front of the bar set, Allison prepared for her turn. She jumped and reached for the low bar. She kept her arms by her ears as she caught the bar and glided out. She brought her toes to the bar, kipped up, leaned her shoulders over the bar, and casted to handstand. She lowered herself down by leaning her shoulders over the bar, kipped out, and casted again, hitting handstand. She did one more, then added her squat-on between the bars, jumped to the high bar and did a long hang kip, cast handstand. She leaned her shoulders over the bar to slow her swing down a little so she could do another kip and casted to handstand again. On the third one, she was just short of handstand, but was pretty close.

Getting off the bar and chalking up in under ten seconds, Allison got on the next empty bar and did another set. Allison was the first in her group to make it through warm-up and on to her workout. She made it a point to always be on an empty bar, and wasted no time getting her assignment done. She looked at the bar workout. Three sets of giants: she decided to do one set on the single rail and a set on each of the competition sets. The single rail was open first. Allison climbed up to the bar, piked her toes to the bar in front and opened her hips and shoulders to get a swing started. She did a kip cast handstand into her giant.

Allison didn't like casting to handstand on the high bar without a kip. The height of the bar bothered her, and she felt uneasy. But if she went directly from a kip, she couldn't focus on how far the floor was away from her, and she was fine.

In her handstand, she looked at the floor as she pushed through her shoulders, and hollowed her body down to where the low bar would be. She arched through the bottom of her swing, and tapped her body to a hollow body so her toes would lead her over the top of the bar back to handstand. Each of her five giants got faster and faster.

"Nice, Allison," Jean said. "Really work on a later tap swing."

"Okay," Allison answered as she chalked up again and got in line at one of the competition sets.

Erica did a kip cast handstand, lowered herself down, and during her glide into her kip, her feet hit the floor. Her next cast was lower, and the third was just above horizontal. Her feet tapped on every kip between handstands. Erica was taller than all of the other girls in the group and these warm-ups proved more difficult for her. Her most recent growth spurt seemed to hit her the hardest so far, as it seemed that her core muscles and hip flexors couldn't keep up with the length of her body. She finished her high bar kips and looked down at the bright red mat burn on her toes. She sprayed water on them and kept going. It was just another day in Paradise.

Allison jumped up on the low bar in a front support, casted up to put her feet on the bar in a squat-on, and jumped to the high bar. Arms by her ears, she caught the bar, swung out, piked her toes to the bar, and kipped up and casted to handstand. Looking at the low bar, Allison hollowed her body past the bar, arched for her tap swing, and swung back up to handstand. She did four more giants to a layout flyaway for her dismount. She landed, finished, and hopped over to the other set of bars to do one more set.

Some could have considered Allison a bar hog, but no one ever complained about her. She always encouraged her teammates, but most of all, she focused on finishing her workout and doing it well. Constantly moving in the gym, Allison, although she had no idea, was an example to even the upper-level girls who saw her as an up and coming force to be reckoned with. Her silent leadership encouraged her teammates to keep moving through their workouts without too much standing around.

Allison finished what would have been her last half pirouette on the competition set. She tapped her toes on the floor coming down from handstand into her kip. "Get your head in, Al, and turn sooner," coached Jean. Allison nodded and got back in line to do a better one.

"Aren't you finished with those?" asked Erica.

"Yeah, but I don't want to end on that one," Allison said as she prepared for her turn. She jumped and reached for the low bar, did a glide kip, cast handstand, and as she straddled her legs for her handstand, she switched her left hand, and turned her body so she finished right in a vertical line as she brought her legs back together. Leaning over her hands a bit, she controlled her swing so she could do another glide kip out to a squat-on.

"That's the way, Al!" cheered Jean. "Work on toe-hechts. I'd love for you to be able to do one directly out of your half pirouette."

"Okay!" said Allison. She went over to the empty rec low bar to set up a drill.

As a reward for finishing their assigned workouts before the end of an event, the girls got to work upgrade skills for the next level. Every workout, Allison tried as much as possible to get her regular workout finished so she could move on and do drills for higher-level skills. Now, this would be even more important with someone like Katie in the gym!

Allison was content working on her own. She never held it over anyone's head when she finished before the rest of the team. The fact that she did so was common to everyone now and they all aspired to be like her. There were a couple of girls who were able to get their workouts completed in a timely fashion and had a few minutes left over to work on new skills, but Allison was a mainstay.

"Nice one, Samantha! Head over and work with Al on toe-hechts," Allison heard Jean say.

"Do you want to grab the noodle and we can hold it for each other?" Samantha asked.

"Yeah," Allison said. She picked up a blue pool noodle and held it over her head in place of a high bar. Samantha casted to handstand, put one foot on the bar, leaned back and put the other foot on the bar, swinging in a pike backwards. After she swung under the bar, she shot her toes up to the ceiling, let go of the bar with her hands, reached for the noodle and landed with a "thud" on her stomach on the mat. This was the drill the two girls did for the rest of bars, the noodle serving as a soft target for the high bar. In the actual skill, the goal was to grab the high bar and be able to kip out.

After event workouts, all of the groups joined together to condition. Allison found Katie. "Do you want to condition with us?" she asked, pointing at Erica. A look of relief passed over the little gymnast's face.

"Thanks. I was worried I would have to condition on my own."

"Of course! You can work with us any time," said Allison.

"How was your first workout at TGC?" asked Erica.

"It went pretty well. I was a little nervous; everyone here is so good and the coaches are pretty tough. It seemed to go all right, though."

"Well, you seem to be doing fine; you'll fit right in," Allison answered.

"Thanks," Katie said as the three started their v-ups.

After conditioning and stretching, the girls filed out to the locker room. As she was leaving, Allison said, "Have a good night, Katie. Hang in there; you're doing great."

"Yeah, and if you ever need anything, we're always here!" Erica added.

"Thanks guys. Bye!" Katie smiled as her mom gave her a hug in the lobby.

When Allison got in the car, her little sister, Morgan, was also in the back seat. "Who is that new girl?" Morgan asked.

"'Hi' to you too," Allison said, rolling her eyes. "Her name is Katie, and she's working in the group below mine. She's *really* good."

"How was practice?" Allison's mom asked.

"It went awesome! On bars Jean had me working toe-hechts. She wants me to do it right out of my half pirouette!" Allison beamed.

"I'm not even going to ask what that is," Allison's dad said.

"That's probably best, Dad," Allison said. They all laughed.

Dear Diary,

Today at practice was amazing! Jean wants me to work a toe-hecht out of my half pirouette! How awesome would that be? That's something that Becca has in her bar routine, and she's a Premier! The new girl, Katie, is nice. She's really good. I have to keep working hard so she doesn't pass me up! Her press handstand is way better than mine - it looks like Liz's! I don't think she will be in her group for very long. I don't even know why she competed level 5 last season at her old gym. She's too good for that. Anyway, I asked her to condition with Erica and me. She seemed to like having somewhere to land. More tomorrow. I have to read for English!

Allison's next day at practice was a little off everywhere. She started on beam, and the assignment was to stick five routines in a row. On her first routine, Allison fell on her back walkover, back handspring. She stuck the second routine with two huge wobbles, then on the third routine, she fell on her full turn! Frustrated, Allison walked over to the water fountain and tried to get her mind and body back on track. She started her next routine: mount, full turn, switch leap, floor. *Not again!* Allison was on her eighth routine when it was time to rotate, and she only stuck two. Not good. However, she knew that she still had three more events to go, so she needed to stay focused.

On to floor, Allison's routine was a little flat. Her first pass was a round-off back half, punch front. She over rotated and rolled forward out of it. Her second pass, a round-off back handspring full, was okay, but she landed with her chest low and she crunched her ankles. On her last pass, a front handspring front pike, she landed short and had to step backwards. It just wasn't her day.

Allison's vault was a pike Tsukahara (or Tsuk). She made it around, but it was not as high as usual. She just felt like she couldn't easily move her body like she normally did. She really started to get frustrated.

"I just want today to be over," she lamented to Erica while they put on their grips. Allison's legs were heavy. She was glad that she didn't have to tumble or vault anymore, but she was tired. Allison made her way through the bar warm-up relatively quickly. The assignment was five full routines, just like on beam.

The first routine was going better than her other events. Her half pirouette finished right on top of the bar, and she kipped nicely out of it. Her swing felt on. She came to the end of her routine, and did her kip, cast, handstand. She let her body fall toward the low bar so she could tap her body over the bar in a giant swing and all of a sudden, her mind went blank. Her wrists didn't rotate over the top of her giant. Her body stopped working, but the momentum kept her body going and Allison came back to the bar, crashing her hip bones against it. She had the feeling of going down a high roller coaster in her stomach. *That was weird. I didn't do my giant.*

"All right, Al. Get up and finish your routine," instructed Jean, calmly.

Allison went to the chalk box, rubbed the block across her grips, and jumped back up on the bar. She barely heard her teammates and little sister, who was on vault, cheer her on as she jumped to the high bar to do her kip, cast, handstand. This time, rather than falling into a normal tap swing, Allison tucked her knees in the handstand and slowed herself down so she wouldn't bang her hips on the bar. She didn't think she could do it. She swung down to the floor. The team stopped cheering and watched as Jean walked over to Allison. Morgan stared in disbelief.

She put her hands on Allison's shoulders and asked, "What's going on, Al? We don't balk in this gym. Are you hurt?"

"No," Allison answered, looking down at the chalk-covered floor.

"Then what's the problem? You already did giants in your warm-up."

"I don't know. Maybe I'm just really tired," Allison started to cry. If the girls in her group weren't paying attention to Allison before, they were now; this was out of character.

"Get a hold of yourself. It's just a weird day. You're tired. Take a minute, get a drink, and do some giants on the single rail."

Allison walked over to the drinking fountain and stood leaning against it with a hand resting on each side. She stared at the "Gym Rules" poster hanging in front of her, trying to get rid of the butterflies that fluttered uncontrollably in her stomach. *What is going on here? Why am I stopping? I'm not doing that again. It was scary!* She looked down at her hips. The red from banging the bar was beginning to turn purple.

"Allison, let's go!" she heard Jean's voice. She chalked up and went over to the single rail. Her hands were shaking a little from the adrenaline rush from when she balked. Allison jumped up to the bar, swung out to do her kip, cast handstand, and she fell over. "Try again!" Jean said. Allison did the same thing two more times, in an attempt to run out the clock on her bar workout. "Allison, you need a break. Go take five minutes and visualize."

Crying, Allison walked to the locker room and sat in the corner on the floor with her knees bent and her elbows resting on them. Her chalky grips dangled in the air. She tried to visualize a giant in her head. All she could see was herself spinning uncontrollably around the bar, bashing her hips on the bar in the process. She didn't try to visualize again. Instead, she cried harder. At that point, Erica walked in the locker room.

"Al, Jean wants you to go back out there. What's going on?"

"I don't know. My mind is blank, and I have no idea how to do a giant anymore."

"Come on, Al. You can do it. You do it everyday. Try not to think so hard."

"How can I not think about it?"

Allison tried to dry her eyes before entering the gym, but was unable to stop her tears. She stood at the chalk box chalking her grips. She walked over to the competition set to start her bar routine. "You can't see through tears, Allison. Let Samantha go ahead of you," Jean said. Samantha had finished her routines and moved on to toe-hechts between the bars. This did not help Allison feel less frustrated. She continued to cry. When it was her turn again, she casted over on the low bar right after her kip mount. Jean was obviously frustrated at this point.

"Allison, what's the problem?"

"I don't think I can do my giant, and now I'm scared of trying, because I think I'll balk and whack my hips again."

"Okay, time is just about up on bars. It was just a weird fluke for the day. Don't worry too much about it, and it will be back to normal next practice."

This made Allison cry even harder, yet again. Next practice wasn't until *Monday*. She had the whole weekend to think about this! Allison couldn't remember the last time she didn't complete a bar workout.

During conditioning, Allison and Erica were doing their sets of leg lifts when Katie came over to ask them if she could work with them.

Erica said, "Of course! How was your workout today?"

"Oh, it was fine. I'm starting to get the hang of the coaches. I'm really sore though. How was your workout?"

Erica looked at Allison who was cranking out leg lifts. "Uh, it was fine." Allison still didn't answer. After her set of ten, she jumped off the bar, went to the chalk box, and went to the next bar to start her sets of military pull-ups.

Katie whispered to Erica in the chalk box, "What's wrong with Allison?"

"Oh, she had a rough day on bars. She wouldn't go for her giant for some reason. Just ignore her. She'll be fine on Monday."

"That's too bad. Her giants are really good."

On the ride home from the gym, Allison's mom asked, as usual, "How was practice?"

"Fine," Allison mumbled.

"It didn't seem 'fine,'" said Morgan.

"Shut up!"

"Hey! Be nice," their mom said.

Allison couldn't tell her mom about bars. It was embarrassing, and she didn't want a lot of questions that she couldn't answer. Allison wanted to go home and sleep. The last thing she wanted was to *talk* about it, and she didn't need Morgan's two cents, either. All she wanted to do was *forget* about it.

Dinner wasn't much better. "How'd practice go tonight, Al?" her dad asked. Did you do that thing you told me about in the car?"

"No. And I'm full," Allison said. "May I please be excused?"

"Sure, honey," answered her mom.

Allison brought her dishes to the sink and went upstairs. "Was it something I said?" her dad asked.

"No. I think she just had a rough day at practice. She'll be fine in the morning, I'm sure," Allison's mom said.

"Al balked on bars and was sent out of the gym," Morgan piped up. "She was crying a lot during practice."

"Did she get hurt?" both parents asked in unison.

"I don't think so. It didn't look like it. But Jean was pretty mad at her."

"Huh," their mom answered. Both parents just looked at each other with puzzled looks on their faces.

Up in her room, behind closed doors, Allison tried to forget about practice. The problem was, though, she couldn't get her giants out of her head. While she lay in bed trying to fall asleep, all she could picture was herself balking and crashing back into the bar. More tears flooded her eyes, and she couldn't sleep.

Dear Diary,

It's 2 am and I can't sleep. I had such a bad workout today, and all I want to do is cry. I didn't go for my giants, and I bashed my hips into the bar. It was the scariest thing I've ever done, and all I want to do is forget about it. But it's the only thing I can think about! Jean told me that I would be back to normal on Monday, but I don't believe her. If it was a fluke, I would have gone for it right after I did that weird baby-giant-smash-into-the-bar thing. What if I don't go for it on Monday? What if I lost my giants? What if I have to scratch bars in the first meet?!?! And if I scratch bars, what's the point of only competing three events? Ugh!

Allison quietly sobbed into the pillow and finally fell asleep at 4 am.

It was ten o'clock before Allison woke up on Sunday morning. She looked in the mirror. Her puffy eyes and tear-stained face gave away just how much sleep she got — or didn't get. It definitely wasn't a bad dream. She went to the bathroom to wash her face. Her mom came down the hallway.

"I thought I heard you get up," she said. "Are you okay?"

"Yeah," Allison answered.

"Do you want to talk about it?"

"There's nothing to talk about."

"Morgan told us what happened at the gym yesterday."

Allison rolled her eyes. It was so annoying having a little sister spying on her all the time. "I don't want to talk about it," she answered.

"Okay, but if you do, you can come to me or your dad. You know that, right?" Her mom gave her a squeeze. Allison gave a half-hearted smile as her mom left the room.

What was she going to do all day today and tomorrow before practice? How was she going to forget about her giants? Allison tried to write her English essay, but she caught herself daydreaming about smashing her hips on the bar. Again, she turned to her diary.

I can't get it out of my head! What if I lost my giants? What if I have to scratch? What if this is it and I can't go any farther? I can't do bars without giants, and I can't compete higher levels without bars! I can't even picture myself going for a giant, let alone a whole bar routine. I don't even want to go to bars tomorrow. What's the point of even going to practice? All I'm going to think about is bars, and the rest of my practice won't be any good. I hate this. I don't even want to go. What's the point?

Eventually, Allison made it through her English essay and it was dark outside. She was caught in a weird place where she wanted the day to be over because she couldn't stop thinking about bars, but she also didn't want tomorrow to come because she didn't want to face bars. It was going too slowly but too fast all at the same time…

At Monday's practice, Allison looked at the schedule. Her group was slated to start on bars. Allison winced. "Hi, Al!" Erica said coming up behind her to look at the schedule.

"Hi," Allison said without enthusiasm.

"What's wrong?"

"Nothing."

"What's wrong?" What did Erica mean, "what's wrong?" I'm not going for my giants! That's "what's wrong!" Allison turned and walked over to the floor and sat in a straddle by herself. Erica's eyes followed her, and she wondered what she did to make her best friend mad.

"Okay, girls! Let's get warmed up!" Jean called. Allison followed everyone else and jogged around the floor. Her face was stoic. She went though the motions of her warm-up, not focused on tight legs, arms, or feet. Jean had to remind her many times to point her toes, something that she never had to do.

At bars, Allison took her time getting her grips on and chalking up, prompting Jean to yell at her to get moving. The workout was five of each skill and five full routines. Allison finished each of her five skills, minus her giants and dismounts. She didn't even want to attempt them, knowing that she wasn't going to go for them.

"All right, Al. Get your giant-dismounts in," said Jean.

Allison didn't answer, but went to the chalk box knowing that she wasn't going to go for the skill.

Katie's group was tumbling on floor. Katie's beautiful round-off, back handspring layout caught Erica and Allison's eye. Erica said to Allison, "Wow, Al, did you see that? Katie's going to be really good!"

Allison was annoyed with Erica's remark. She wanted to be comforted; she didn't want to have to think about how good some little twerp was. She was mad! By this time, it was her turn on the bar. "Come on, Al!" her teammates cheered. She didn't go; she casted over on her handstand.

"Get up and go again," Jean said. Allison did the same thing.

Not knowing what else to do at this point, Jean told Allison to go back into the locker room and think about it some more. Allison saw no point in thinking about it. If she wasn't going to go for her giants, why even bother? She just wanted to give up; this was embarrassing.

Allison pouted her way to the locker room, tears streaming down her face. She sat in the locker room crying until her teammates came to put their grips away. Slowly, she took her grips off and stuffed her grip bag in her locker. She went out to do beam with the rest of her team.

"Allison," said Jean, "I know you're frustrated. But I know you can do your giants. You should know that you can do them. Don't you believe that you can?"

"I don't know anymore," Allison answered quietly.

"Well, until you decide that you can do it, you're not going to be able to. Gymnastics is mental." She pointed to her temple then walked away.

Allison put her hands over her eyes and cried harder. Erica came over and put her arm around Allison. "It's okay, Al. It'll come back."

"I'm not so sure," Allison said.

Allison scowled her way through the rest of practice. By the end, she didn't even know how she did. She was just going through the motions. All she could think about was bars and how she couldn't believe that this was happening to her.

At practice the next day, the younger kids were on bars. They worked giants on the single rail. Allison was so mad at them, especially at Katie. Hers were perfect, of course. Allison didn't even want to be at gymnastics now. Maybe she should just quit. It would certainly be easier than this torture!

When Allison's group finished stretching, they went to floor. Again, Allison didn't do very well. Her mind wasn't with it; all she could think about was bars, and the fact that she just didn't want to be there. They were doing floor routines, and Allison hadn't performed one that poorly all year. "Think about what you're doing, Allison!" Jean yelled. "You're just doing it to get it done!"

The next two events were beam and vault. Allison just wasn't concentrating. She couldn't do her vault or stay on the beam. She was really frustrated. So was Jean.

Of course, by the time they went to bars, Allison just wasn't in the mood. Again, she had the feeling that she couldn't do her giants. She tried to avoid them the best as possible, but, of course, Jean caught on. She told Allison that she had to try some giants, maybe on the single rail. Allison didn't want to, but she knew that she should at least make it look like she was trying.

Allison got up on the bar, did a kip cast handstand, and went blank. She slowed herself down and went around the bar back to her hips. It happened again! Allison was so frustrated now that everyone in the gym knew there was something wrong with her. She was bawling.

Jean told Allison to go sit out and calm down. Allison didn't see the point of sitting out and thinking more about something that wasn't happening, but it was better than humiliating herself in front of the whole gym again. She stayed in the locker room as long as possible, until Jean came to get her and tell her to join the rest of the team for conditioning. *She's so mad at me, she won't even talk to me*, thought Allison. But at the same time, she was relieved. She really didn't want to talk about something she couldn't explain.

During conditioning, Erica told Allison that she had talked to Katie. She also said that Katie had been watching Allison since she first came to the gym. Katie really thought highly of Allison and wished she wouldn't be so sad. Her giants would come back.

"What does she know? She's only nine," snapped Allison. Erica glared at her best friend and told her that she was being unfair; Katie was just trying to be nice.

"I'm going over to condition with her. I don't know what your problem is, but you don't have to take it out on everyone else."

Allison was surprised and angry at Erica's comment. At this point, all she needed was her best friend to comfort her and help her through her problem. But Erica didn't even want to condition with her; she was taking the new girl's side. Allison conditioned on her own, fuming at Erica and Katie, as the two of them chatted and worked together.

While the team stretched, Allison was still on her own. She lowered her head as Jean came over and said, "Allison, I know you're frustrated. Believe it or not, I'm just as frustrated as you are. I don't know why you're not going or where your block came from. All I do know is that you are better than to let something like this get in your way and affect your other events, your mood, and your teammates. The fact is, being a good gymnast is more than just loving the sport and doing your best when things are going your way. The true test of character is how you handle it when things aren't going well. I don't know how much more I can help you but to tell you that you're not going to overcome this mental block until you get it in your mind and believe that it is over and that you are going to do your giant. Know that you are fully capable of performing a giant and then *quit thinking*. Let your body do its work. I can believe in you all I want, but until you believe it, you're not going to go. Go home and get psyched up. Visualize yourself doing your giants over and over again. I don't want you on bars at all until you *know* that you are ready to go. All right?"

Allison looked up at Jean. *What?! I'm not allowed on bars at all?*

"All right," she answered.

"Grab your mom before you leave so I can talk to her a little bit."

Allison and her mom walked into Jean's office. "Allison, do you mind waiting outside?" Jean asked. Allison silently turned around and closed the door behind her.

I can't believe they're in there talking about me, she thought as she sat on the bench on the lobby.

"Al's having a hard time, isn't she?" Allison's mom began.

"She has a mental block on her giant," Jean said.

"What does that mean, exactly?"

"It means that, for whatever reason, she's not going for the skill. Nothing in particular happened that would make her balk, but she just won't go. Sometimes the cause is just a lack of trust in herself and her ability, or sometimes it's the brain's way of reacting to muscle memory. Most of what a gymnast does is automatic. Sometimes, if her brain tries to concentrate on it, it's almost unfathomable for it to break the skill down and understand it. In any case, things get muddy, and she just can't go."

"Well, what do we do for her?"

"I have told Allison that I don't want her back on bars until she is sure that she is going to go for it."

"How can she be sure? And how can that be good — to avoid it?"

"By visualizing. Right now, if you ask her if she can see herself going, she will say 'no.' The first step in physically going is mentally going — not avoiding — mentally working."

"What can I do?"

"Unfortunately, not much, and, actually, the less you do, probably the better. Allison is obsessing about this, if she is like any other gymnast. It's all she can think about. It's hard and frustrating. Just give her time and understanding — even if you don't understand! If she comes to you to talk, just listen. Remind her that she is awesome and that she needs to believe in herself. That's really all that can be done. It is truly up to her."

"Well, okay. Thanks for the talk, Jean. I'll try to be cool."

"Thank you for your support," Jean smiled.

Jean and Allison's mom came out of the office. "Have a good night, kid." Jean patted Allison on the shoulder as she walked away.

In the car, Allison's mom said, "Al, Jean filled me in on what's going on. I just want you to know that I back her up. If she says that not doing bars for awhile will help you, then I can only believe that it will. I know you probably don't want to talk about it, but if you ever get to the point that you do, I'm here for you. I believe in you, Sweetie. So does Jean."

“Thanks, Mom,” Allison responded.

Allison thought about what Jean had said earlier. Of course, Allison wanted to go for her giants and keep getting better in the gym. Of course she knew that she *could* do her giants. At the same time, she was upset that Jean took bars away from her, but she was also relieved that she didn’t have to go to bars until she was ready. Maybe she’d never go back…*No, I have to do bars. I have to figure this out.*

Before she went to sleep, Allison said to herself, “Okay, this is it. I know I can do a giant. I’ve been doing them for two years.” Allison closed her eyes and tried to visualize a giant. Again, she saw herself balk. She opened her eyes, shook her head, and started over. She did this until she forced her brain to visualize herself completing a giant. Once she got it, she kept trying. Sometimes she would see herself doing her giant, and then other times she saw herself balk. Before she fell asleep, she made a decision.

Mental Block

Before warm-up the next day at practice, Allison found Jean. "Jean, can I talk to you?"

"Sure, Al. What's up?"

"First, I want to apologize for how I've acted. I haven't been trying my hardest, and I haven't been a good teammate or role model."

"I understand, and you're forgiven," Jean said. "Gymnastics is mental. It's so hard to believe in yourself when things aren't going your way. But it's times like these when you learn your greatest lessons."

Allison swallowed hard. She didn't know how to ask this, but she had a plan. The worst thing that could happen is that Jean would say no. "Can I skip bars today?" she blurted out.

"You don't think it's in there?" Jean asked.

"Well, last night, I was finally able to visualize myself doing my giant without epic failure. But I couldn't see it all the time. I was wondering if I could not do bars today, focus on my other events, and work on visualizing it some more until I get it consistent."

"Do you think it will work?" Jean asked.

"Yes, I do," Allison answered with conviction.

"Me, too," smiled Jean. "Why don't you spend half of bars visualizing and the other half doing physical abilities?"

"That sounds good," Allison said. "Thank you, Jean."

"You're welcome, Al. Believe it or not, I want it as much as you do."

Allison's group went to beam first. With the weight of bars off her shoulders, Allison was able to fully concentrate on her routines. She finally felt like herself. In fact, she finished her workout and even got to work aerials again!

Bars was next. Allison found a quiet corner in the gym and sat to visualize her giants. She still had to force herself to see herself being successful, but she did it, and watched herself many times. Her hands got a little sweaty, and she felt a little nervous in her stomach. She was starting to believe that she could do it.

The rest of her workout went well. Allison felt like she was back to normal on vault and floor. She was much happier, and much more herself. Erica didn't spend much time with Allison during practice, but Allison didn't push it. She wanted to focus on getting herself back on track. They weren't ignoring each other, they just didn't spend much time together.

Allison went home with a better attitude.

"How was practice today?" her mom asked.

"Better. I didn't do bars," Al answered.

"Not at all?" her mom asked, a bit surprised. A part of her thought that Al would just go for her giant today, rather than face not doing the event.

"Don't worry," Allison said. "It's all part of the plan."

"Okay," her mom said with a nod of her head.

Mental Block

Dear Diary,

I had a much better practice today. I was nervous, but I asked Jean if I could not do bars today so I could focus on my other events and not worry so much about my giant. In the mean time, I spent my time visualizing and making myself picture my giants in my head. I'm feeling much more confident now, and I'm ready to try to go tomorrow! Every time I visualize, I can see myself doing my giants the right way. I get a little nervous when I'm picturing them, just like I would at a meet. I think I'm ready to go. I hope to do them tomorrow, and I'm gonna try to do this!

All for now. Next time I write, I'll have tried my giants!

At the gym, Allison's group started on floor. Allison's routines went well, and she really was confident and felt ready for the competition season.

Beam was next. The assignment was to stick four routines or do eight. It took Allison five routines to stick four, which wasn't bad.

Vault was next, meaning bars was last. Allison started to really get nervous. She couldn't fully concentrate on her vaults because all she could think about was her giants. *The pressure is on.* Allison wondered if today was going to be the day or not. She was about to find out. "Girls! Go to bars!" yelled Jean.

"Allison, what's the prognosis today?" asked Jean.

"Well, I'd like to *try* my giants today."

"No," said Jean. "You're not ready."

"But can't I at least see if I can do it?"

"Nope. Not today. You're not 100 percent confident. Our deal was no bars until you *know* that you'll go."

Allison could feel tears filling up her eyes. "Okay," she answered. "What should I do instead?"

"You should do what you did yesterday — visualize and physical abilities. You'll get there, Al. Be patient."

Patient?! Was Jean crazy? This is getting ridiculous!

Despite the fact that Allison was upset with Jean for telling her she wasn't ready, she was a bit relieved that she didn't have to go to bars today. Maybe Jean was right...

Mental Block

Dear Diary,

I thought that I was going to go for my giant today, but by the time we got to bars, I started freaking out a little bit. As practice went on, I could only think about giants and wondering if I was going to go. Jean wouldn't let me go because she said I wasn't confident. It's true - I wasn't confident. But I will be tomorrow. I'm going to go for my giants! I've decided that enough is enough. I'm ready to do what I can see when I visualize it. I'm going to go for my giants tomorrow! Tomorrow is the day! Off to visualize! Next time I write, I'll have done my giants!

Allison was excited to get to bars and not only try but *do* her giants. She had three full routines to get done after her warm-up. Allison got through her kip cast handstands and tap swings, taking everything one skill at a time. Giants were next. Before she mounted the bar, Allison took a deep breath and visualized herself completing her giant. She opened her eyes, got up on the bar, and jumped to the high bar. She did a kip, cast handstand, fell toward the low bar, tapped her body, switched her hands over the top and did a giant! She continued her set of five and did a flyaway to get off the bar. Everyone cheered. Jean gave her a high-five and Allison beamed from ear to ear. She let out a huge sign of relief. *Wow*, she thought. *I did it!*

In the chalk box, Erica said, "Nice job, Al. I knew you could do it."

"Thanks, Erica. I'm sorry I was such a brat."

"It's okay. You were going through a rough spot. I guess I didn't know how to help you through it."

During conditioning, Allison and Erica asked Katie if she would like to join them. As they caught their breath between their sprints, Allison said to Katie, "You know, you're really good. I'll bet in no time you'll be working out on Saturdays with us."

"Wow; do you think so? I would love to work with the upper-level girls!"

Allison smiled at Katie, making the little gymnast feel more and more welcome in the gym.

"Good job on your giants today, Allison," Katie said. "It was as though you never lost them."

"Thanks. They were there the whole time. It was a really frustrating week. I even thought about quitting! But Jean helped me to understand that I just had to take a step back and make my brain work for me, and not against me. I feel a whole lot better now!"

Dear Diary,

I went for my giants! I have them back! I did them multiple times, and I have them back! I feel SO MUCH BETTER! It was strange that Jean had me stay off of bars for a couple of days just to visualize and stuff, but it really took the pressure off me. I was able to go to the other events and do what I know how to do. It made me more confident! And now I can do my giants again! Woo hoo!

The next day at practice was Saturday, when Allison and other selected gymnasts worked out with the upper-level girls to prime them for the upcoming skills and competitive years of gymnastics. Allison's workout went very well. She worked double back drills on floor and Yurochenko drills on vault. On bars, as she was warming up, she had just a little bit of a nervous feeling when it came to do her giants, but she knew that she would go for them anyway. After her first set, Jim, her coach for the day, told her to go one the single rail and start working drills for blind changes. Allison smiled as she chalked up and gladly got in line.

Author Biography

Mary (Reiss) Farias grew up in Minnesota as the youngest of eleven children. When she started doing gymnastics at the age of five, her coaches saw potential in her strong muscles and ability. They quickly moved her along to pre team, and then up to competitive team.

Mary competed under both USA Gymnastics (USAG) and US Association of Independent Gymnastics Clubs (USAIGC). She became a national competitor in both leagues, earning her a full athletic scholarship to the University of Arizona in Tucson.

Mary stayed in Tucson and has since opened a gym with her husband, Marc, called Tucson Gymnastics Center. There, they are proud to train both recreational and competitive gymnasts, including their own daughter, under intelligent rules that USAIGC provides.

The author of the children's book series "Gym Rats," Mary's goal is to show that gymnastics is more than just the ability to flip and twist. She is passionate about teaching children life lessons through the great sport.

Made in the USA
Monee, IL
07 April 2021

65007722R00030